W9-BLI-864

MARSHMALLOW

MARSH

STORY AND

CLARE TURL

MALLOW

PICTURES BY
AY NEWBERRY

HarperCollins*Publishers*

Copyright © 2008 by Felicia Noelle Trujillo

Printed in the United States of America.
All rights reserved. No part of this book may be used or reproduced in any manner whatso-
ever without written permission except in the case of brief quotations embodied in critical
articles and reviews. For information address HarperCollins Children's Books, a division of
HarperCollins Publishers, 1350 Avenue of the Americas, New York, NY 10019.
www.harpercollinschildrens.com

Library of Congress Cataloging-in-Publication Data is available.
ISBN-10: 0-06-072486-2 (trade bdg.) — ISBN-13: 978-0-06-072486-3 (trade bdg.)
ISBN-10: 0-06-072487-0 (lib. bdg.) — ISBN-13: 978-0-06-072487-0 (lib. bdg.)

Typography by Stephanie Bart-Horvath
2 3 4 5 6 7 8 9 10
❖
Revised Edition
Adapted from *Marshmallow*, © 1942, renewed 1990, by Clare Turlay Newberry

For Ellen Kearns

Oliver was a gray cat with tabby markings who lived in an apartment. Many a cat has to catch his dinner before he can eat it, but Oliver was lucky. When he was hungry, all he had to do was mention the fact to Miss Tilly, and she would open the refrigerator and get out his liver or chopped beef.

Peace and quiet was what he wanted

As Oliver never went out, he did not know that the world was full of other animals. The only mice in his life were gray flannel ones filled with catnip, and the nearest thing to a rabbit he had ever seen was a stuffed plush Easter bunny.

But Oliver did not care. Peace and quiet was what he wanted, and his meals on time.

Life, however, cannot always be like that. One day Miss Tilly called him from the kitchen.

"Prr'owrr!" replied Oliver, and he hurried over, expecting to find his dinner.

Instead, Miss Tilly was smiling at something she held in her two cupped hands. It was small and white and furry.

"What do you think of this, Oliver?" she said. "Its name is Marshmallow." She held the furry thing to her cheek for a moment, then set it on the floor.

It had tall ears, pink eyes, a wiggly nose, and twitchy whiskers. And it was *alive*!

Oliver was appalled. He took one wild look at the creature, then squinched his eyes tight shut.

"Oliver, what is the matter with you?" cried Miss Tilly. "Don't tell me you're afraid of a little tiny baby bunny!"

But Oliver *was* afraid. He was too frightened even to run away, but crouched in a corner, opening and closing his eyes as if it actually hurt them to look at a rabbit.

As for Marshmallow, he was a very unhappy little bunny. All he wanted was to be at home again with his nice warm furry mother.

If he had been a kitten, he would have mewed. If he had been a puppy, he would have howled. And if he had been a baby, he would have cried his eyes out. But being a bunny, he just sat still and felt sad.

However, Marshmallow cheered up a bit when he had his dinner—a raw carrot and a bowl of rolled oats. The bowl said D O G on it, for the shop did not have any dishes with R A B B I T or B U N N Y on them. But as Marshmallow could not read, this did not much matter.

He ate the green carrot-top first, for he was thirsty. Then he munched part of the carrot. After that he tried the rolled oats, eating with little quick nibbles, *crunch-crunch-crunch*. When he had finished eating, he hopped into the bowl and took a nap!

That night Marshmallow slept in the bathroom on a bed made out of a folded towel. It was not the same as having a soft furry mother to cuddle against. Still he did not cry.

Nor did he yowl for his breakfast the next morning.

"If only you were nice and quiet like that, Oliver," yawned Miss Tilly when Oliver woke her with frantic scratchings and meowings at her bedroom door.

Miss Tilly warmed some chopped beef for him, gave Marshmallow another carrot, and made herself some coffee and toast. Then she sat down at her typewriter and wrote

A POEM IN PRAISE OF RABBITS

A bunny is a quiet pet,
A bunny is the best thing yet,
A bunny never makes a sound,
A bunny's nice to have around.

Puppies whimper, bark, and growl;
Kittens mew, and tomcats yowl;
Birdies twitter, chirp, and tweet;
Moo-cows moo, and lambkins bleat;

Some creatures bellow, others bray;
Some hoot or honk, or yap, or neigh;
Most creatures make annoying noises,
Even little girls and boyses.

A bunny, though, is never heard,
He simply never says a word.
A bunny's a delightful habit,
No home's complete without a rabbit.

That morning Oliver felt much braver. He hardly squinched his eyes at all when he looked at the bunny now, and by afternoon he was watching Marshmallow with an expression that would have terrified an older and wiser rabbit.

Marshmallow, however, was like a tiny new baby that scarcely noticed what went on. He ate when he was hungry and the rest of the time he slept, with his paws tucked up under him to keep them warm.

Oliver began creeping toward the sleeping bunny, his eyes glaring wickedly. But just as he got ready to spring, Miss Tilly cried, "Oliver! Don't you dare hurt that bunny!"

Oliver sat up, blinking innocently.

"This just isn't going to work out," Miss Tilly told herself sadly. "Cats always have hunted rabbits, and I suppose they always will." She put Oliver in the other room, and after that she did not let him come near Marshmallow.

Soon Marshmallow began lolloping about the apartment, sniffing things, and then tasting them. And nearly everything seemed to taste pretty good.

He nibbled the rugs, working very hard in one place until he had gnawed a little bare spot before moving on. He stood on his hind legs and yanked books out of the bookcase. He chewed the chair and table legs. And every time Miss Tilly sat down for a moment, he came hopping up cheerfully to untie her shoelaces. He was a very busy little bunny. Miss Tilly was surprised to find that he nibbled so many things besides carrots. She wrote another poem on her typewriter, which she called

A SOLEMN WARNING
TO RABBIT LOVERS

A bunny nibbles all day long,
A bunny doesn't think it's wrong.
He nibbles mittens, mufflers, mops,
He only pauses when he hops.
He nibbles curtains, lamp-cords, shoes,
He only stops to take a snooze.

Sofa pillow, ribbons, rugs—
He takes a mouthful, then he tugs.
Galoshes, boxes, books, and string—
A bunny nibbles everything.

One afternoon Miss Tilly stayed out later than usual. When Oliver woke from his nap there was no dinner waiting for him, so he trotted to the door of the other room and said, "Prr'owrr!"

There was no answer, but he could hear odd sounds in the next room, small scuffling noises that caused his eyes to widen and his ears to point suddenly forward. These sounds were made by Marshmallow's little feet, as he went lippity-lippity around the room.

Marshmallow had discovered Miss Tilly's old plush Easter bunny and had thoroughly nibbled its whiskers. Now he was just frolicking about the room and kicking up his heels for sheer joy of being alive.

Oliver was listening and sniffing while his eyes grew bigger and bigger.

"Prr'owrr!" he said again, and scratched impatiently at the door. When this did no good, he stood up on his hind legs and patted the doorknob. Finally he reached up both forepaws, and with one on each side of the knob he worked it this way and that. At last there was a small *click*, the door swung open, and Oliver padded silently into the next room.

And there was that rabbit, skipping about as if he hadn't a care in the world.

He would dash several feet in one direction, stop suddenly, and spring into the air. Then he would turn, dash back to his starting point, and jump again, back and forth, back and forth.

Oliver watched it with great interest. Each time the little rabbit whisked by him he lashed his tail and got ready to spring.

But somehow he couldn't quite do it. Perhaps he remembered that Miss Tilly had told him not to hurt the bunny, or perhaps he was still just a bit afraid.

Suddenly Marshmallow sat up tall and stared at the cat, his soft nose twitching rapidly. He looked most inquisitive but not in the least alarmed.

Marshmallow sat up tall

What was this great striped animal, he wondered? Could it possibly be his mother in a new coat?

And while Oliver hesitated, trying to make up his mind to pounce, all at once Marshmallow scampered joyfully up to him and kissed him on the nose!

Marshmallow shut his eyes and snuggled close, blissfully happy to have found another furry animal.

Even when Oliver opened his jaws and took hold of him with his teeth, Marshmallow was not afraid. For the next moment Oliver was licking his face as tenderly as any mother cat with her kitten. And like any mother cat he licked the fur in the wrong direction, so that it stood on end and looked all mussed up.

He licked the fur in the wrong direction

The bunny cuddled up to him

After that Miss Tilly let them play together every day, for she saw that they were friends. They romped like two kittens, and wherever the cat went Marshmallow followed, lippity-lippity, right at his heels. And whenever Oliver lay down to take a nap, the bunny cuddled up to him as close as he could get.

Oliver forgot that he had ever thought of Marshmallow as a strange animal to be pounced upon. He adopted the little bunny and brought him up as his own kitten. And although Oliver never said so, I cannot help thinking that in time he came to agree with Miss Tilly that . . .

A bunny's a delightful habit,

No home's complete without a rabbit.

Brighten your home with a bunny,

He's fat, he's frisky, he's funny.

He's soft, he's downy,

He's cute, he's clown-y,

Oh, brighten your home with a bunny!